WELCOME TO
PASSPORT TO READING
A beginning reader's ticket to a brand-new world!

Every book in this program is designed to build read-along and read-alone skills, level by level, through engaging and enriching stories. As the reader turns each page, he or she will become more confident with new vocabulary, sight words, and comprehension.

These PASSPORT TO READING levels will help you choose the perfect book for every reader.

READING TOGETHER
Read short words in simple sentence structures together to begin a reader's journey.

READING OUT LOUD
Encourage developing readers to sound out words in more complex stories with simple vocabulary.

READING INDEPENDENTLY
Newly independent readers gain confidence reading more complex sentences with higher word counts.

READY TO READ MORE
Readers prepare for chapter books with fewer illustrations and longer paragraphs.

This book features sight words from the educator-supported w Sight Words List. This encourages the reader to recognize commonly used vocabulary words, increasing reading speed and fluency.

For more information, please visit passporttoreadingbooks.com.

Enjoy the journey!

Little, Brown and Company

Hachette Book Group
1290 Avenue of the Americas, New York, NY 10104
Visit us at lb-kids.com

Little, Brown and Company is a division of Hachette Book Group, Inc.
The Little, Brown name and logo are trademarks of Hachette Book Group, Inc.

The publisher is not responsible for websites (or their content) that are not owned by the publisher.

First Edition: April 2016

Library of Congress Control Number: 2015947167

ISBN 978-0-316-26078-7

10 9 8 7 6 5

CW

Printed in the United States of America

Passport to Reading titles are leveled by independent reviewers applying the standards developed by Irene Fountas and Gay Su Pinnell in *Matching Books to Readers: Using Leveled Books in Guided Reading*, Heinemann, 1999.

DreamWorks

DINOTRUX
TO THE
RESCUE!

Adapted by
Emily Sollinger

L B

LITTLE, BROWN AND COMPANY
New York   Boston

Attention, DINOTRUX fans!
Look for these characters
when you read this book.
Can you spot them all?

Ty

Ton-Ton

Dozer

Revvit

Ton-Ton and Ty were playing catch. Ton-Ton jumped for the rock.

Ton-Ton flipped over.

One of his parts fell off.

"We will get you fixed," said Ty.

"We will go to the repair shop."

"Oh, yeah!" said Ton-Ton

The Reptools worked hard.

They fixed Ton-Ton.

He was ready to play again!

"A Scraptor!" called Dozer from outside.

"We will help you, Dozer!" said Ty.

"We are on our way."
Ty, Ton-Ton, and Skya
rushed outside to help.

"Big mistake, Scraptor dude!"
said Ton-Ton.

The Scraptor chased the
Dinotrux and Reptools.

Ty trapped the Scraptor
with two big rocks.

He put the Scraptor
in Ton-Ton's bed.

Ton-Ton drove very fast.
Ton-Ton drove very far.

He tossed the Scraptor over a cliff.

"And don't come back!" Ton-Ton yelled.

Oh no!

A big pack of Scraptors appeared.

They dragged Ton-Ton to their scrapyard.

Ton-Ton noticed another Dinotrux.

"I am Ton-Ton," he said.

"I am George," said the Dozeratops.

Skya, Dozer, Ty, and Revvit
worried about Ton-Ton.

"I will look for him," said Ty.

"I will come with you," said Revvit.

"I miss that dude."

They found Ton-Ton's tracks!
Ty, Revvit, Skya, and Dozer followed
the tracks.

They made it to the scrapyard.
The Scraptors were asleep.

The Dinotrux crept inside.

Ton-Ton was happy to see his friends.

"We have to save George, too," he said.

"We have enough parts to fix you both,"
said Revvit.

The Dinotrux worked quickly.
They worked quietly.

While Ton-Ton was being fixed,
he started to giggle.
"It tickles!" he laughed.

Ton-Ton's giggle woke the Scraptors.

"Run for it!" said Ty.

The Scraptors caught up quickly.

They blocked the exit.

"How will we get out?" asked Dozer.

"We will build a tunnel," said Ty.

The Dinotrux worked together.
They built a tunnel.

They made it to the other side.

The Scraptors were getting closer.

Ty used his wrecking ball.

Rocks and dirt crashed down.

The tunnel caved in.

The Scraptors were trapped.

"Hooray! We did it!" cheered the Dinotrux.

"Boom!" said Ty.
"Scrap that!"